MW00806857

The Magical Soul

By: Marisela Marquez

Illustrated by:
Nadia Ronquillo

ISBN: 978-1-7368878-8-2

Printed and published by Ingramspark, 2021

DEDICATION:

In memory of all those who have gone before us, especially my dear Alex, Dad, Baby and beloved pets. May you all be dancing in Heaven, awaiting our magical souls.

To my beautiful baby girl, may you continue to rise like the sun every day, even when life seems dark and uncertain. I am honored to be your Mama to walk this journey hand in hand with you.

And to all the children in the world who lost their parent(s) too soon. May you all live life to the fullest to tell your stories one day up in Heaven.

Love,
MM

Meet Marie, a beautiful, smart girl filled with curiosity.

One thing she was curious about was her Papa. She often wondered about him since he was no longer living. She knew her Papa had died when she was younger, but where was he now?

Marie's curiosity grew stronger and stronger as she got older. What is curiosity, you might ask?

Curiosity is when you have the desire to learn more about something.
Marie was full of questions.
She wanted to know more about everything!

So one day, Marie decided to start asking questions.

Marie asked, her face full of wonder.

Mama, tell me
about Papa.
Where is he now?

Everything!

Marie shouted.

"When Papa found out that we were expecting you, his eyes lit up with so much love and joy. He wanted to be the best Papa in the whole wide world, and he was."

"He loved hearing you laugh and seeing your eyes light up when you saw him. You made Papa very happy," said Mama.

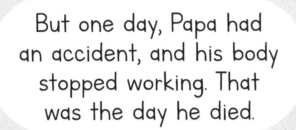

But one day, Papa had an accident, and his body stopped working. That was the day he died.

Mama explained as she kissed Marie squarely on the forehead.

"Well, my dear child," said Mama, "the body can stop working and die when it suffers trauma either from an accident, an illness, or even just because of old age. Sometimes Doctors can make it better, but sometimes they can't. So the body ends up dying. But when the body dies, **THE MAGICAL SOUL** is set free and finds its way to Heaven."

Mama paused for a moment and wrapped her arms a bit tighter around Marie, showing her how much love she had to give.

"That is where Papa is now. Heaven is a beautiful and magical place. A place where God lives, with all of our loved ones that have moved on from Earth."

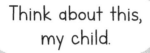

Think about this, my child.

Mama proceeded.

People have two magical parts, the first magical part, is your body, you can see it with your eyes. You can touch your body, feel your body, and move your body.

20

The second magical part you cannot see at all, but it's inside of you. It's called a soul, **THE MAGICAL SOUL**, Mama explained.

Marie's eyes opened wider. She wanted to know more.

Tell me more about THE MAGICAL SOUL Mama!

22

Her Mama looked down at her and smiled. "THE MAGICAL SOUL, is a combination of all the parts of who you are as a person. It is a unique mixture of your special personality, your thoughts, and your love. Your soul is what goes up to Heaven and lives there forever. From Heaven, our loved ones can watch over us, listen to us, and guide us."

"Even though you won't be able to hear his voice, you can ask him for advice, tell him about your day, or even just let him know you miss him. Go ahead, talk to him." She urged, "He will listen. He may answer you in a dream, in a vision, in a feeling, or simply in a choice you make.

His **MAGICAL SOUL** is listening all the time. All our loved ones are there listening if we need them, even our beloved pets who no longer live here on Earth with us."

Hearing this made Marie very happy, because she knew her Papa was watching over her even though she could not see him or hear him.

Mama then told Marie, "love never dies, and our love for each other and for Papa will live on forever. This is the best part of the MAGIC of the SOUL."

Marie smiled as this thought filled her up with warmth.

But for now, we need to learn as much as we can, laugh often, cry when we need to, and enjoy life here as much as possible. When it's your **MAGICAL SOUL'S** turn to go, you will take so many stories with you to Heaven, so you can tell all of our loved ones in detail about your time spent here on Earth.

Author's Note:

One of the most challenging things any parent or guardian can do is have a conversation about death with a child. This scenario is what inspired me to write The Magical Soul Book.

A few years ago, I lost my father, husband, and I had a miscarriage, all within four months, right after leaving my corporate career. I was in my early 30's shell shocked, broken-hearted, and needing to raise a 13-month-old daughter.

How was I going to do this?

I knew I could not change the fact that our daughter would grow up without her father and sibling. But I did have a choice on how we were going to integrate our losses into life. For most people, death is an uncomfortable topic to discuss, especially with children. Yet, it is something that undoubtedly will affect us all.

One of the most helpful things I found to be in my journey was learning more about the soul or our energy. We know that energy cannot be destroyed, and religious beliefs indicate that we are more than just a body. It was vital for me to share this information with our daughter in a child-like form.

I created this book to inspire hope, comfort, and connection for grieving children and provide an invitation for adults wanting to discuss death with children. Death is a reality that will affect us all at one point or another. Still, our Magical Soul cannot be destroyed and therefore lives on forever!

Thank you for sharing this magic with me!
Love,
Marisela Marquez

Founder of embracingwidowhood.com and The Embracing Widowhood Podcast.

CPSIA information can be obtained
at www.ICGtesting.com
Printed in the USA
LVHW071706120621
690059LV00006BA/555